Zenobia Orimoloye

IMPRESSIONS
Up Close and Personal Short Stories

IMPRESSIONS
Up Close and Personal Short Stories

Zenobia Orimoloye

CITI OF BOOKS

Copyright © 2024 by Zenobia Orimoloye

All rights reserved. No part of this publication may be reproduced, distributed, or transmitted in any form or by any means, including, photocopying,recording, or other electronic or mechanical methods, without the prior written permission of the copyright owner and the publisher, except in the case of brief quotations embodied in critical reviews and certain other noncommercial uses permitted by copyright law. For permission requests, write to the publisher, addressed "Attention: Permissions Coordinator," at the address below.

CITIOFBOOKS, INC.
3736 Eubank NE Suite A1
Albuquerque, NM 87111-3579
www.citiofbooks.com
Hotline: 1 (877) 389-2759
Fax: 1 (505) 930-7244

Ordering Information:
Quantity sales. Special discounts are available on quantity purchases by corporations, associations, and others. For details, contact the publisher at the address above.

Printed in the United States of America.
ISBN-13:	Paperback	979-8-89391-399-6
	eBook	979-8-89391-400-9

Library of Congress Control Number: 2024921520

Contents

A Sunny Day 1
Brothers 4
Dilemma 14
Henrietta 19
Home 22
Night Shift 24
The Obituary 27
Serendipity 30
Six o'clock News 34
Struggling 36
Tested 39
Why Me 41
Family 47
Hollywood 51
Justice 54
Last Hurrah 57
Law & Order 61
Missing 74
Temptation 78
The Front 81
Poetry Musings 85
Old and New 85
About the Author 88

Passages

A Sunny Day

The incident happened when I was about nine or ten years old. It's hard to remember exactly because it occurred so long ago. It was summertime, and school was out until September. It was a warm sunny day in Chicago.

My mom and I lived across the street from a park. She and my dad separated after I was born. My grandma said they didn't need to be together because they fought too much. They were teenagers when they had me.

I wanted to go out and play with the other kids. As an only child, I loved to be around other kids, especially my age group. We played hop-scotch, dodgeball, "Captain, May I?" and we jumped double-dutch. I was good at double-dutch. But my mom wouldn't let me go out. She wanted me to stay with her to keep her company.

On that sunny day, I looked out the window and watched the kids playing and having fun. I didn't want to stay in with her. My mom was moody that day; she put on her favorite jazz record and played it over and over as she sat on the sofa looking sad. I was sick of hearing it. She was usually playful, but not today.

Thank goodness she stopped playing the record. But then she sat down and started to cry. I'd never seen her cry before.

She moaned, "Nobody loves me. I'm tired of being broke. I miss my momma and daddy. I'm lonely. I need some help."

I didn't know what to do. I looked for one of her favorite records. Green Onions by Booker T. & the MG's. She loved that recording, and even made up a dance to go with it. She'd do the dance at family gatherings, and everyone would clap for her. She was always happy when she heard that record. I found it, but she wouldn't let me play it.

I just sat in the chair staring at her. 1 wanted to go outside because it was a sunny day. I was mad and tired of her crying. All of a sudden, she stopped crying. She had this funny look on her face. She told me I was smart, like my dad, and she was proud to have a smart daughter like me.

She went to the bathroom, then came back into the living room. She told me I could go outside. I got ready to go outside when I noticed something. She had pills in her hand and swallowed them with a big glass of water. She told me she was going to bed, and I could play outside as long as I wanted. She got into bed, pulling the sheet over her face. I don't why, but she was scaring me. A funny feeling came over me.

I called my Aunt Constance. I told her my mom had taken some pills, gone to bed in the middle of the day, and pulled the sheet over her face.

My aunt shouted, "Oh, shit. Get her out of bed now! Don't let her go to sleep. Give her some water and milk. Make her stick her finger down her throat until she throws up!"

I did as instructed. I dragged her out of bed. I walked her around the apartment for hours. She threw up several times. I sat her in the chair and played Green Onions for her.

She seemed better, but I wouldn't let her lie down. She sat in the chair as I watched her all night. She smiled at me.

She whispered, "At least I have you."

That was the day I stopped my mom from committing suicide.

Brothers

It's a warm summer evening in Morgan Park, a southside community in Chicago. Janet and Mary are two sisters who live together in a three-bedroom home in this neighborhood. They are schoolteachers and very close. Mary is engaged to Ted. Janet has dated Larry for two years. Larry and Ted are best friends. The sisters haven't heard from their men for two days.

Janet: It's hot outside. Good thing we got the AC fixed. Have you seen Larry?

Mary: No, I haven't seen him.

Janet: I called Larry and texted him, but no response. That's not like him. I talk to him every day. I haven't heard from him in two days.

Mary: Now that you mention it, I haven't heard from Ted either. We don't talk every day, but sometimes he'll text me. Let me check my text messages.

Janet: I'll call his sister Rose to see if she's heard from him. I'll buzz her now. [*Dials phone*] Hi, Rose. How you doing? By the way, have you seen your brother Larry?

Rose: No, I haven't seen him since last week. You know he don't call me every day.

Janet: I haven't heard from him in two days, Rose. If you hear from him, tell him to call me.

Mary: 1 checked my messages, nothing from Ted. I wonder where he could be. It's not like him to not text, even if he don't call. I try not to be one of those clinging girlfriends, where he has to call me every day.

Janet: Are you calling me clinging?

Mary: No. Larry loves calling you every day. Besides, he started calling every day, not you. He has spoiled you. Always calling you his queen and buying you flowers. I hope he pops the question soon so you can get your ring and stop staring at mine.

Janet: I'll call his job in the morning. He never misses work, especially now that he's trying to get that promotion.

Janet: [*Calls Larry's job*] Hi, Pam. May I speak to Larry? You haven't heard from him in two days?

Janet: Mary, please call Ted's job to see if he knows anything about Larry.

Mary: Hi, Ann. Is Ted in? Oh, he hasn't been to work in two days? Okay, bye.

Mary: I just got a text from Fay. She says Ray hasn't called her in two days. Tliey had an argument, but she thought Ray would be over it by now. Fay called his job, and they haven't heard from him in two days.

Janet: Okay, something isn't right. No one has heard from Larry, Ted, or Ray in two days. None of them have gone to work. It's not like them to miss work. Should we call the police since they have been missing for forty-eight hours?

Mary: Let's have a family meeting, then decide what to do.

Janet: No, I want to call the police right now. I'm scared for them. Forget calling, we can go by the police station since it's not that far.

[Mary and Janet leave the house and drive to the police station. When they arrive, they run up the steps, enter the building, and stop by the front desk]

Mary: I don't like coming to the station. It makes me nervous.

Janet: It's for a worthy purpose.

[As Janet looks around, she sees people she knows from the neighborhood. There's Jean, Carol, Mr. Johnson, and Fred. Janet waves at them to come over to where she and her sister are standing]

Johson: My son hasn't been home in two days. He missed work, and that's not like him. He loves being a fireman. We are here to file a missing person's report. "The guys in their families are missing too.

Mary: We came because Ted, Larry, and Ray are missing. [*Mary bites her nails*]

Janet: [*Talks to the officer at the front desk*] May I speak to Captain Ed Jones? He's a family friend.

Officer: Let me check to see if the Captain is available.

Captain Jones: [*Comes out of his office. Walks over to the group and escorts Janet and Mary into his office*] It's always a pleasure to see you two. What can I do for you?

Janet: Ed, we are concerned. Larry, my boyfriend, Ray, our brother, and Ted, Mary's fiancé, have been missing for two days. Can you help us?

Captain Jones: Can you two come to a neighborhood meeting tonight because I'm going to address this issue. Something is going on. I must admit I did not take it seriously until now.

Janet: What changed your mind?

Captain Jones: My brother is missing. His wife is frantic. She thinks somebody has killed him. My parents think he's been in an accident. They are worried sick. Now I'm worried too.

Mary: Ed, what can we do to help?

Captain Jones: I've been getting phone calls from people in the neighborhood about missing husbands, boyfriends, uncles, brothers, friends, etc. I need you to contact as many people as you can to tell them to come to tonight's meeting. I will give you a list of names of people calling about missing persons. My staff will give you whatever assistance you need.

Janet: We'll make and pass out flyers using the people we know. We'll contact other teachers, since they're off for the summer like us. Don't worry, Ed. You know that when the Bryant sisters take on a task, we get it done!!

Captain Jones: Thank you, ladies. The meeting will be held at the Ada Park Field House at 7:00 p.m.

Janet: We'll notify the Mayor's Office and our alderman.

Also, we'll contact the local newspapers. We'll need their help too.

Captain Jones: I have a reporter friend. I'll contact him. We'll also check with other cities.

Janet: This is a serious matter. Something smells funny. We need to mobilize now. We got to deal with this quickly. The public must be made aware that this is not just a coincidence. Our men are missing!

[*As they open the door to leave Ed's office, they hear loud voices. The police station is filled with an angry crowd of people demanding to speak to someone regarding missing male relatives. Women are crying and men are shouting that they need assistance now. The phones are ringing off the hook as people continue to call in about missing men. Mary's phone vibrates, indicating a text message. She looks down at the messaged*]

> THEY HAVE CAPTURED US.
> WE NEED HELP!!!!!!!

Mary grabs her phone and texts back, "Where are you?" The response: "Crawdaddy s Kitchen at 9370 Mansfield Rd in Shreveport. Ask for Big Al."

Mary and Janet fall back in their chairs, glad to hear some news. Captain Ed Jones changes plans. He cancels the meeting at Ada Park until he can see where this text will lead. He tells the concerned groups at the station to go home. He will contact them once he has concrete information. He calls in his senior officers to give them an update on the situation. They can also hear the call to Big Al, along with the Bryant sisters.

There's tension in the air as he makes the call to Big Al.

The person answering the phone mumbles, "Big Al ain't here," and hangs up before Ed can respond. Ed is pissed now. He calls back. The same person answers again.

Ed threatens, "This is a life and death issue. I need to talk to someone in charge. Tell them the FBI's calling."

There's a loud commotion in the background as someone shouts for Zita to pick up the phone. Captain Jones identifies himself, stating he needs to talk to Big Al immediately. Zita takes his number, promising she will have Big Al call as soon as possible. They sit there, anxiously waiting for the call. Mary sobs into her hands.

Ten minutes later, the phone rings. It's Big Al. Ed identifies himself as a Chicago Police Department captain. Big Al says, "I thought you were with the FBI."

"We'll talk about that later/' Ed says.

"The guy who had me send the text said he had two sisters. What're their names, Captain?"

"Mary and Janet Bryant, and their brother's Ray/' Ed says.

Janet shouts, "We're here now. Where's my brother?" Mary stops crying.

Big Al begins his story: "Yesterday, while I was in the men's room, a white man came in, looked around, and brought this black guy in to use it. The guy stood there as the black guy peed. I thought, 'Man, he can't even pee in peace. Must be some police shit.' I walked out, going to the kitchen area, when the black guy walking behind me tripped and knocked me down. It was kind of noisy, but he whispered quickly in my ear, 'Ray Bryant, Chicago, sisters Mary and Janet, they have captured us, we need help!' I picked him up as he stumbled outside with the white guy. I noticed the white guy handcuff him and throw him in the back of a big white truck with a Nevada license plate. I used Zabasearch.com to get the phone numbers of the sisters."

Relief floods the room because they know Ray is alive for now. Ed thanks Big Al for his help, explaining that he doesn't have any jurisdiction in Louisiana and needs to talk to someone at the police department down there.

Big Al tells him, "Sergeant Remy Broussard can help you."

Ed explains, "We must act quickly because they kidnapped black men from our neighborhood. We gotta find them."

Big Al says, "I'll be goddamned. Slavery again?! Hell no! Give Remy a call. He's a Cajun, a good guy, well respected, and connected down here. He can track down anything. It's in his blood."

Ed and Remy talk for an hour with everybody listening on speaker phone.

Ed tells him, "I'll fly down there tonight."

"I'll pick you up at the airport," Remy says.

Mary tears up again, and Janet hugs her. Ed tells his staff to stay on alert, sending the sisters home to get some rest. He'll keep them informed once he gets there. Everybody reluctantly leaves his office.

Sergeant Remy Broussard goes to work. He tells the deputies to skip the hotels, and instead concentrate on RV parks like Tall Pines, Lakewood Village, Country Haven, Kampgrounds of America, especially Gavel Falls Campground, because they're near Caddo Lake, where people do a lot of fishing and hunting. It's a more secluded area too.

The staff gets busy. Remy's in charge since the higherups are attending a conference in New Orleans.

One deputy hits pay dirt when he talks to the owner of Gavel Falls. The owner states that a white truck with Nevada plates came in the day before, with plans to leave the following morning. Remy tells the guys to be at the site by 5:00 a.m.

Remy calls Ed to tell him they located the white truck.

"See you in a couple of hours," Ed says. "I'll go with you for the morning raid. I'll be the tall black man in a red shirt wearing a Chicago Bulls cap."

When he arrives, Remy picks up Ed and takes him to the Shreveport station. They discuss the situation and their options. On a hunch, Remy decides to go out to Gavel Falls that night instead of waiting until the morning. He and Ed load up and get there about midnight. They drink coffee to stay alert. Around 2:00 a.m., they hear a noise. The white truck is moving, but it stops when the police car pulls out in front.

Remy jumps out of the car, firing two shots in the air to get their attention. Remy takes the driver's side as Ed runs to the passenger side, their AR-15s ready for action. The two guys in the truck are shaking and offer no resistance. Once they're handcuffed, Remy gets the keys and opens the back of the truck. A sea of black faces look terrified and weary.

"Ray, are you there?" Ed shouts.

There's a muffled sound, a cough, and then a voice yells, "Thank you, Jesus."

Men file out of the truck, falling on their knees, crying out of pure joy of being found. Ed searches familiar faces with his flashlight, and then he sees them: Ted, Larry, Ray, and his brother. They all come together in one giant hug.

"Y'all need a bath," Ed says. Remy calls for backup. Thirty minutes later, the deputies come with a school bus for the victims and a squad car for the two thugs. They get back to the station about 3:30 a.m.

Remy puts a call in to an FBI guy he knows, asking him to come to the station to interrogate the kidnappers and interview the fifty black male victims.

Ed puts in a call to the Bryant sisters. The phones picked up on the first ring. It's Janet. She hears, "Hey, baby girl," and knows it's her brother. Then she hears, "How's my queen?" She yells to Mary that the guys are all right.

They have so many questions, but have to wait because the men are tired and dehydrated. Ed says, "You can talk to them later. We'll be home soon."

Four FBI special agents arrive at 9:00 a.m. to question the two thugs. The agents scare the shit out of them, saying they could get the death penalty. They spill their guts. They nervously explain that they were transporters picking up cargo from one point to deliver to the next site, which was Beaumont, Texas. This batch was going for the screening process listed below to determine their use:

1. Recent or prolonged incarceration, institutionalization or homelessness.
2. Check for communicable diseases, such as HIV/Aids or Hepatitis B or C.
3. History of intravenous (IV) drug use.
4. Overweight or underweight.

Once the screenings were completed, the men would be categorized to be sold for use as organ donors or whole-body donors. There's a need for healthy organs and cadavers for scientific research across the globe. This is a lucrative business. The network of smugglers have a European distribution facility and two full-service facilities on the West Coast.

"We don't kill anybody/' the arrested men confess. "We only transport the cargo."

This operation has been in existence for years. That's all they know.

The two criminals are eager to cooperate, hoping to get lighter sentences. They agree to work with the FBI to capture these human traffickers and shut down their operation.

Three of the agents stay behind to interview the victims. Remy arranges for the group to get food and showers and phone calls to contact their families. These men are the lucky ones.

Ed talks to the rescued men, who inform him that the two thugs said the men were targeted because nobody cares about missing "niggers." Ed smiles at the group. "As you can see, those assholes were wrong. You're going home!"

Dilemma

I BROKE UP WITH my girlfriend Crystal after two years of being the perfect power couple. She's high-maintenance, and she was getting on my nerves. She was on the mayor's staff, making good money.

We got invited to all the important parties, which was good for me, since I was an attorney with one of the big law firms. She's all about appearances, the fancy car, designer bags, and clothes. She spent money like it was water, but her father always covers for her when she overspends. She's spoiled rotten. Her motto is: if you got it, flaunt it.

Crystal's mother and my mother were sorority sisters in their college days. Both mothers thought Crystal and I were ideal matches because we had similar backgrounds. Crystal graduated from the University of Chicago. I got my BA from Morehouse and my law degree from Yale. They wanted Crystal to become my wife, Mrs. Harold Davis. They wanted me to go into politics like my dad. After all, Crystal would be a great politician's wife. Crystal is stunning. She's light-skinned with green eyes, naturally long chestnut hair with a great figure she keeps up by working out at the gym five times a week. Her family's from a long line of Creoles out of Louisiana. My family came from Georgia during the great migration of Blacks moving from the south to the north for a better life. We're living the American dream.

I should've been happy. I had a great job, a beautiful woman, and money in the bank. But sometimes I felt there should be more to life. Something was missing. There was no passion in my life. I did all the right things, such as church on Sundays, networking with other professionals, and volunteering for pro bono work at the Legal Aid Clinic.

I was working one of those cases when I met Yolanda Allen. She brought her brother down to get a lawyer to help him with child support issues. He wanted to make arrangements to start paying again. I helped him complete the necessary paperwork and set up a court date for him. While I was helping her brother, I'd sneak at look at her. Yolanda had beautiful white teeth, brown flawless skin, and she wore a short afro accented with large gold hoop earrings. She had large breasts, which also caught my eye. Every time she caught me looking at her, she'd roll her eyes and wrinkle her cute nose.

She left with her brother after an hour-long session. She thanked me, saying she'd be there with him in court. I told them to be sure to be on time. I gave her my card in case they had any questions. I sat at the desk thinking about her, especially her perfume. It lingered in the air after she left.

Three weeks later, we met in court. Everything went well. Yolanda's brother hurriedly left the courtroom with his new girlfriend. As Yolanda was leaving, I said, "Let's celebrate with a latte at Starbucks." She agreed.

We went there and stayed for two hours, just talking. She's single, twenty-five, and likes her job with an IT firm. She's a graduate of Loyola University, with a bachelor's degree in business and a minor in computer science.

Since we both worked in downtown Chicago, we started meeting two or three times a week for lunch. Finally, I asked her for a date. We went to movies, plays, bowling, jazz clubs, and bike riding. We had fun together, liking many of the same things. I couldn't believe my good fortune. Yolanda is special. I monopolized all of her free time because I enjoyed being with her. I'm content when she's around. We really got to know each other; I didn't mind that we weren't having sex.

Yolanda invited me over for dinner one Saturday evening. We ate baked salmon, string beans, and corn, with peach cobbler as dessert. It was a good meal that ended with cocktails.

I leaned over to kiss her, and it turned into a long, sensual kiss as she ran her tongue over my lips and sucked my tongue. I moaned. "Can I stay the night?" I asked.

She took off her blouse, then her bra while still kissing me. We fell on the floor, stopped to take off our clothes, and rushed to the bedroom. She sucked my nipples, which was a new experience for me. It felt great! I licked her all over. It was a night of hot passion. I hadn't felt this alive in years.

The next morning, I looked at her as she slept. I didn't go to church that day. She woke up, stuck her tongue out, and wiggled it at me. It made me horny, and we went at it again. We spent the whole day in bed. By evening, I was exhausted but joyful.

We became a couple. I'd found my soulmate. She ran my bath water, gave me massages and pedicures, and willingly cooked. I bought her flowers weekly and got her anything she wanted. She crooned, "All I want or need is you." Damn, I'm hooked. She's the woman I want in my life permanently. Yolanda stimulates my mind and body!

I stopped going to church and Sunday family dinners. My mom called me at work, saying she needed me to come this Sunday because some family personal business came up. I told her I wanted the family to meet Yolanda, a special person in my life. Mom said she could meet her later, when it wasn't a private meeting with the family.

I agreed to wait for a later date and informed Yolanda that soon she'd meet my family. She said she was also taking her time before she introduced me to her family because she wanted to see if the relationship lasted. We've been together four months and plan on moving in together. We admitted that we're in love, with marriage in our future. Life is good for us!

I arrived Sunday at 1:00 p.m. at my parents' home. Mom and Dad were sitting in the living room. Dad had a stern look on his face. Mom directed me to sit on the sofa. I smiled at both of them, asking where my brother and sister were, since it was a family meeting. I heard footsteps coming down the stairs. It was Crystal, followed by her mom and her dad, Judge Bowler.

I was stunned to see her 'cause I hadn't seen her in months. My mom directed her to sit down by me. She said Crystal had something to tell me.

Crystal whispered, "Well, Mr. Harold Davis, I'm going to have your baby. I'm four months along. I was going to tell you the night you ended our relationship, but I was too upset about the break-up to say anything at that time. I planned on having an abortion, but I couldn't do it." She placed my hand on her swollen belly.

My father spoke. "Sometimes these things happen, son. We raised you to be a man who takes responsibility for his actions. Now it's up to you to do the right thing by Crystal."

I mumbled, "I don't love her anymore."

My father said, "You did at one time, you can love her again. She's carrying our bloodline. This is our first grandchild."

My mother chimed in. "You can get married now before she gets bigger. I'll make all the arrangements. Crystal can move into your two-bedroom condo until you get a house." I looked at Crystal for help.

She smiled. "Harold, it's going to be all right. You're just going through a phase. I still love you. We'll be great parents."

I had a sinking feeling in my gut as they planned my future. I told them I needed time to think about it. Judge Bowler chuckled. "Let me share something with you," he said. "My wife was pregnant when I married her, and it worked out fine. We've been together thirty-five years. It's time to take action. You and my daughter have a bright future ahead. I have the utmost respect for you. Are you going to do right by her?"

I sat there like a trapped rat as all eyes were glued on me, waiting for my decision!

Henrietta

WE LIVED IN a close-knit neighborhood on the southside of Chicago. I was twelve years old at the time, with an older sister, Roberta, who was named after our dad, Robert.

Usually, I was with Roberta and her friends, who were two years older. They didn't want me around, but my sister was my babysitter. If she wanted to go somewhere, she had to take me. Anyway, she liked having me around. I looked up to her and could keep secrets.

It was fun being around the older girls. You got to hear a lot of stuff. It made me feel grown up. Roberta wasn't so bad; she was just boy crazy. She and her friends constantly talked about the boys they liked. I would sit and listen as they talked about Boo Boo, Junior, JB, and Duck. We would always go over Gloria's house because she had brothers who were friends with those guys.

Things changed in our neighborhood when a new family moved down the street from us.

The Banks family had two kids. Henrietta and her brother, Dennis, who was my age. Her brother was kind of cute with his big afro. Henrietta was brown-skinned with pearly white teeth. She had a big booty, small waist, and breasts larger than my mom's. My sister and her friends didn't like her. They said she was stuck up. Most of the girls didn't like her because the boys were crazy for Henrietta. Roberta told me that Henrietta showed out at a party. It made the girls mad. I liked Henrietta because she was friendly and always joking with everybody.

Henrietta was always the belle of all the parties. I heard my sister tell her friends, "Don't invite her to the party next Saturday." It didn't matter because the boys brought Henrietta with them. Although she wasn't pretty like my sister, she looked okay. She was the most popular girl with the boys, especially Tyrone and his friends. My sister was invited to a birthday party for Gloria's brother Tyrone. Of course, I got to tag along. I was excited because this was my first time being allowed to attend a party with Roberta.

We arrived at Gloria's house and went down in the basement where the party was being held. The decorations were colorful, with Tyrone's name spelled out in big blue letters. There was loud music playing. Roberta warned me, "Sit down and stay put!"

I found a good spot where I could see the dance floor. It was kind of boring because nobody was dancing, just standing in groups talking. Suddenly, I heard footsteps coming down the stairs; there was Henrietta in a red halter top and a black mini skirt. She waved at me and sauntered over to Tyrone, pulling him on the dance floor. Thue first time I saw Henrietta do it, I was stunned. I'd never seen anything like it. She rolled her stomach like a belly dancer while rotating her butt cheeks like bouncing balls. She would shake her hips from side to side with little jerking motions, which made her breasts bob up and down to the beat of the music. It was a sight to behold. The crowd clapped and chanted, "Go Etta go! Go Etta go!"

Now I know why the guys liked dancing with her. There was a lot of movement going on, especially for the slow songs. I sat there the whole night watching Henrietta in amazement. She got all the attention that night. Now I know why the girls didn't like her.

A year later, her family moved away. Every now and then, I think about Henrietta. I wonder what happened to her.

Home

Home can be a feeling or a place, but for me it's a feeling because 1 have lived in several cities. There was Chicago, Austin, Knoxville, Milwaukee, Cincinnati, and Detroit. Each city had something unique about it.

The neighborhood 1 live in now has been changing since I moved in ten years ago. At first, it was a new subdivision with 150 homes that were affordable. It was quietly under the radar, but now it's a high-profile area. We were discovered, and now our land is valuable to developers.

There's construction on every corner, where before there were open spaces with trees. Our trees have been destroyed to build condos, townhomes, lofts, and apartment buildings. Our streets are narrowed to allow for bicycle paths. Traffic is congested due to more people moving into the area. The East Side is a desirable place to live now. I live five minutes from downtown, ten minutes from the University of Texas, and fifteen minutes from the airport.

Progress is good, but sometimes it erodes the character of a neighborhood. East Austin was an area populated with predominantly minority families for decades, but now that's changing. I enjoy the services of a booming community, but the gentrification cost us more in property taxes.

Ah yes, gentrification, the buying and renovation of houses and stores in deteriorated urban neighborhoods by upper- or middle-income families or individuals, raising property values but often displacing low-income or fixed-income families and small businesses. The houses in my area are no longer affordable for a lot of people. Some of them can't afford to pay their rising property taxes.

I get ads, emails, and phone calls daily from realtors and investors who want to buy my single-story, three-bedroom, two-bathroom house. A friend of mine was offered a million dollars for her two properties in a part of East Austin that's now been renamed Central Austin. She declined the offer because the houses have sentimental value, since they were built by her father, who passed them on to her.

This is happening all over the country as people move closer to the city. They can walk to restaurants, ride their bikes, and lessen their travel time to work. I enjoy watching people attend the University of Texas football games and their tailgating parties since I don't live far from the stadium. Historically, it's difficult to stop progress once it's started. There are advantages and disadvantages to it, but what can you do? You attend meetings to discuss the changes and raise your concerns, but the money people have more clout with City Hall.

It'll be interesting to see how the area looks five years from now if I'm still here. Who knows, someone may make me an offer I can't refuse!!

Night Shift

IT WAS ONE of those days. My car wouldn't start again. I had to catch the bus to get to work. It's obvious I need a new car. I'll need to make some extra money to get enough to put a down payment on a new one. I could borrow the money from my uncle, but I'd have to pay him back with interest because I still owe him money from a prior loan1 which he's bugging me to pay. My other option is to get a second job, which I don't want to -do. I'll try some temp agencies first.

I was on the phone talking to my sister Irene about needing some extra cash. She said the hospital where her friend works was hiring for the night shift. She referred me to her friend Joy1 who could put in a good word for me with her boss. Joy walked me through the process1 told me what to do and say at the interview.

I was hired for the night shift, from 6:00 p.m. to 1:00 a.m., having to work two weekends a month. I have enough time to leave one job at 5:00 p.m. and get to my second one by 6:00 p.m. I'll work it until I have enough money. Since my car isn't reliable, I'll take the bus to both jobs.

The one obstacle is that the bus stop is four blocks from my apartment. The streetlights are usually busted from the kids throwing rocks at them for sport. The streets are dark at 1:30 a.m.

I decided to get me a gun since I would be walking home that late at night. I took the course and got my concealed carry certification. I felt better now. I started the night shift two weeks later. It was a forty-minute bus ride from the night job to my house. Usually, I got off the bus and ran the four blocks home, but the running got to be a bit much, so I just starting walking fast.

After two months of working at the hospital, I had enough money for a good down payment. I decided to leave the job, giving my two-week notice. Joy said I should stay because having a car would make it easier for me, and I could use the extra money to pay off my car sooner. But the two jobs were wearing me down, leaving me little time for myself. Joy told me to think about just working part-time on the weekends.

I was thinking about this as I walked to my house. I was a block from home when I saw a guy walking towards me. Since it was one of those cold, windy Chicago nights, he had on a hoodie with his head down. I was bundled up too, with a wool scarf tied around my face. Immediately, I was on alert. I thought about crossing the street, but that would show fear. He had on some yellow shoes, which caught my eye. I was looking down at the shoes. As he passed me, he grabbed my purse. The gun was in my hand by my side. 1 shot him, running the rest of the way to my apartment.

I stumbled up the stairs, my heart racing, my hands shaking, and my body trembling. I didn't know if I should call the police to report it. I looked out the window and didn't see anybody. No one was on the street. I drank four glasses to calm my nerves. Finally, I went to sleep. The next morning at 7:00 a.m., I got a call from Irene, who had been at the University of Chicago Hospital all night with her daughter. She cried, "Eva, sorry to wake you, but Lateefa came home bleeding because somebody shot her. It was probably one of those damn gangs. She's in surgery now. There was blood all over her new yellow shoes. Get here as soon as you can." I gazed longingly at the empty wine bottle.

The Obituary

The funeral was for Uncle Henry, my mom's brother. The usher gave me a colorful program before I was seated. I found a comfortable spot in the back since I didn't want to view the body. Also, it allowed me to leave quickly. I read the program in my hand.

Celebration of Life
January 20, 1930-August 30, 1985

Henry Robert Jones
Friday, September 9, 1985
Wake 10:00 a.m.
Funeral 11:00 a.m.

AA Rayner and Sons Funeral Home
318 E. 71st Street
Chicago, Illinois 60619

Order of Service
Internment
Pall Bearers
Acknowledgements

Seats for family members were reserved in the front, but I sat in the back. The summary of Uncle Henry's life was in those four paragraphs printed on the program. Henry Robert Jones, known as Hank to his friends, was born in Macon, Georgia, on January 20, 1930, to Minnie and Paul Jones. Henry was the second oldest of five children. Henry's parents relocated to Chicago when he was a young boy.

He was educated in the Chicago public school system, graduating from Paul Laurence Dunbar High School in 1948. He was a veteran of the Korean War. He worked for one of the largest hotel chains in Chicago. He was a bartender by trade. He was married for more than thirty years to his high school sweetheart, Donna Martin Jones. I skimmed over the program because I knew most of it. The ceremony progressed as each speaker walked to the podium to make their remarks. As they praised my uncle, I closed my eyes, thinking about him.

The loving husband who constantly cheated on his wife throughout the marriage. He gave her gonorrhea while she was pregnant. He didn't even have the decency to tell her. She was informed by the Public Health Department, going there alone for treatments. He didn't allow her to wear pants, even in the cold months. He stopped her from attending church, so she would sneak and go on the Sundays he worked. He could be abusive too. He slapped her one time. Because she was light skinned, there was a red mark on her face. I watched her cry. I knew then that I never wanted a man to hit me.

The devoted father of four daughters (Alberta, Velma, Narva, and Thelma), who all married the first man to ask them so they could get out of that house. Two of them married while in high school. Henry didn't talk to Velma for three years, nor acknowledge his grandson, because she had him out of wedlock. He forbids her from coming to the house. She would only visit when he was at work.

We had fun when he wasn't around. He finally talked to Velma again, accepting his grandson after she married the baby's father. He never ate dinner with his family. My aunt would fix his plate first and take it to the bedroom so he could eat alone. His daughters couldn't walk on the same side of the street as a tavern or bar. They had to cross the street to pass one. They did this even though he wasn't around. Boy, we did a lot of crossing the streets. He ruled his family with an iron fist. My cousins had strict rules to follow.

Uncle Henry made the same comments every time he saw me. "Are you gaining weight?" or "How much do you weigh now?" He made me self-conscious, so I avoided him as much as possible. He never said one kind word to me my whole life.

I visited him once when he was sick. He laughed. "Girl, you sure are getting big. You better start pushing away from the table!" Uncle Henry enjoyed tormenting me about my weight. All of his daughters were slim.

I opened my eyes when the ceremony was over. I hugged my aunt and joked with my cousins. We teased their mother for buying Uncle Henry a $200 pair of shoes to wear in the casket. He never had shoes that expensive, but that was his death request, to be buried in those shoes with a new suit. She complied with his wishes. Aunt Donna was a loving and obedient wife.

As I left the funeral home, I threw that damn obituary in the trash.

Serendipity

It started off a gloomy day. It got worse by 4:30 p.m., when I was laid off from my job of five years due to downsizing. I didn't feel like cooking, so I bought pizza for me and my son Kyle. He's twelve years old, and he means the world to me. His father died in a car accident when he was five. The two of us are on our own. I'm an only child, and my parents are dead. I have enough savings for two months of living expenses, which will give me time to find a job.

I stopped at Mrs. Johnson's house to pick up Kyle. She's crazy about him and don't mind keeping him after school. Her grandkids live in another state. As I drove home, I told Kyle about losing my job.

He chuckled, "Mom, you didn't like that job anyway. You're smart. You'll find a better one." That's my boy. He's so positive and upbeat. I devote my time to my son and my job. No time for dating, since being a single mom is challenging.

Looking for employment is exhausting. I forwarded my resume to temp agencies, and lots of opportunities I found online. I have a bachelor's degree from the University of Texas at Austin. I only had two interviews in one month, but no job offers. I like my neighborhood and wanted to keep my two-bedroom, two-bath apartment.

It was the beginning of the second month with no job. Kyle had completed his homework and gone to take the garbage out about thirty minutes before.

I looked out the window. He was talking to a man. I shouted, "Kyle Bailey, get in this house now."

Kyle waved bye to the man and ran up the stairs. I asked, "Who's that man?"

Kyle said, "He's the neighborhood drunk. He's harmless. He tells stories about his time in the military. He also recites poetry by Langston Hughes and Gwendolyn Brooks. He's really smart. I think his experiences in the war made him a drunk."

It was a week later when Kyle yelled for me to come downstairs. The drunk fell and needed help getting up. He looked terrible with his bloodshot eyes. He groaned, "Take me to the VA hospital."

It was an hour's drive, but I took him. I found his ID and got him signed in. His name was Don Pearce. He was forty years old. We left him there and went home.

Two weeks later, a VA social worker called me. She asked, "Are you Ruth Bailey?" I said yes, and she replied, "You need to come and get Don. Since you signed him in, you need to sign him out. Sorry, but that's the rule."

I told her that I didn't want to get involved.

"Too late. You're involved. Come get him tomorrow at noon." She hung up before I could respond.

Damn, I have my own problems. My money is low; rent is due in two weeks. I'll pick him up, but then I'm through with him.

Kyle and I go get him. He looks much better. He's about six feet tall and brown skinned with hazel eyes. His eyes are clear, and he looks decent.

He walked out of the VA a sober man. I just wanted to take him home and get rid of him. Kyle sat in the back seat with him, holding his hand. We didn't talk until we got to our neighborhood. I asked for directions to his house, which was two blocks over from my apartment building. It was a residential area in East Austin. I dropped him off at his house, which clearly needed some work. The lawn needed cutting and the house needed painting. He thanked me and walked slowly to his front door.

Well, I'm still jobless. I'm living out my security and must be out of the apartment by the end of the month. My money is gone. I'm worried but trying to keep up a good front for my son. He's been quiet and secretive ever since the incident with Don. I guess that had an effect on him.

I was sitting in the kitchen with a headache, biting my nails when the doorbell rang. Kyle ran to answer it before I could get up. It was a sober Don. I was startled to see him because I had put him out of my mind. Kyle was holding his hand as he led him to the kitchen table to sit down next to me. Don and Kyle were staring intently at me. The two of them were up to something.

Don spoke first. "Kyle told me about your circumstances. I'm sorry to hear about your predicament. Maybe I can help since you helped me."

I blurted out1 "I don't need your pity. How can a drunk help me? Kyle shouldn't have told you our business."

Kyle was crying now. "Mom, we need help. I don't want to be homeless. I like my school and my friends in this neighborhood. I don't care what you say. We need help. Please listen to Don."

I was so ashamed. I just sat there biting my nails while

Don talked.

Don mumbled. "I know you don't know me, but I wouldn't hurt you or Kyle. Here's my offer. I have a three-bedroom, two-bath house that you and Kyle can share with me until you get on your feet. I'm attending AA meetings for my alcoholism. You can stay as long as you want. I won't bother you. I like Kyle and enjoy seeing him when he stops by to look at some of my books. I'm a disabled vet getting a monthly check, so we'll have food to eat. My deceased parents left me their paid-for house."

I had no pride left. I was desperate as I listened to a stranger offer me a place to live. I accepted his offer with the intent to get the hell out as soon as possible. We moved in two weeks later, after I went over to his house to clean and paint before we moved in.

It's a nice house, once we cleaned it up.

Nine months later, and we haven't left. It's hard to leave with Don begging us to stay. He's thoughtful and well-mannered. He thanks me profusely for anything I do for him, whether it's cooking or washing his clothes. He teases me constantly. He always reads poetry to me after dinner. He beats me at Scrabble all the time. I don't mind losing because he gives me a big hug along with a kiss on my forehead when he wins. I enjoy his company.

Saturday is our movie day. We hold hands and share popcorn during the movie. Life is good with Don. Kyle's a good influence on Don. With the help of AA, Don is staying sober, working at the VA as a counselor for other vets. He's excellent at his job. I'm working now, too. By the way, Don and 1 are getting married next month.

It's been five years. Don is still sober. We have a daughter now. Don adopted Kyle, and they're very close. He's the best father and husband. I can't imagine life without Don.

Six o'clock News

Ms. Mary is a seventy-year-old senior everyone knew in the neighborhood. She's lived in her house for over forty years. Her husband died, her kids moved away but return for holidays and her birthday. Ms. Mary's in good shape for an older lady. She minds her own business except if you interfere with her watching the six o'clock news. She'd shout; "It's time for my news, y'all making too much noise, move away from my window." If she's talking to someone, she'd end the conversation so she can get in the house in time for her news program. It was like an obsession with her. Once, she ruined a dice game because in her rush to see the news, she stomped on the dice. Another time, she called the police on her nextdoor neighbors, who were fighting, requesting the police come and arrest them before her news came on. She was a sweet little lady as long as you didn't interfere with her news program.

Ms. Mary has a routine of shopping on Thursday, which is coupon day. She goes to the same store because she knows where everything's located. Also, all the salesclerks know her. They wave at her as she strolls down the aisles, picking up stocked items, reading the labels, checking the expiration dates.

Ms. Mary fell a month ago, so she's walking with a slight limp but still moving pretty good; it takes longer to heal those old bones. She stops to chit-chat with the clerks. This particular day, she let time get away from her. Once she noticed the time, she started to rush because she didn't want to miss the news.

She had one of the guys take her groceries to the car. She thanked him and gave him a nice tip. She has a generous heart. The clerk went back into the store, not waiting until she got into her car because this was considered a safe area.

Ms. Mary turned toward the driver's side of the car as she looked in her purse for her keys. Usually, she had them out before she got to the car, but in her rush, she didn't do it. She found them. As she put the car key in the lock, a hand grabbed her shoulder. It startled her. As she turned around, she came face to face with a big guy with bad breath in a red jacket with a knife pointing at her. He demanded that she give him her car.

She whined, "I'm a senior on a fixed income, I need my car to get around."

He growled, "Shut up, you old bitch. Give me your car before I hurt you. Now, give me the damn keys."

Ms. Mary threw the keys over his head. He stooped down to get them off the ground. By this time, Ms. Mary pulled a handgun out of her coat pocket. She smirked, "Freeze, scumbag." He lunged at her. She shot him.

He fell to the ground clutching her keys. She yelled for help, and people came running from the store. The police were called. Ms. Mary had to go to the police station to give a statement. Guess who was on the six o'clock news that night!

Struggling

I BEGAN SPIRALING downward after that terrible night in the bar. My brother, Morris, came in, saw me, and came over to where I was sitting. He was tipsy as he started to berate me. He pointed his finger in my face as he shouted, "You killed our momma, bitch. Any fool should've known not to give liquor to a sick person in the hospital. I know you said she begged you, but she did the same thing to us, and we refused. Thank God the lady in the next bed didn't die when you gave her a taste. 1 know the doctors said Momma didn't have long to live, but you hurried it. I hate the sight of you."

By this time, everyone was staring at me. I grabbed my purse and rushed out of the bar crying hysterically. He always did this to me when he saw me, ever since Momma died. He made me feel guilty and ashamed. I wanted to die.

As I was stumbling down the street, someone ran up behind me. A guy caught up with me, grabbing my hand and rubbing it softly. He gave me his handkerchief, saying his name was David Nelson. He steered me to another bar around the corner called the Do Drop In and got us a booth in the back.

He sat me down and kept rubbing my hand. It was soothing. I stopped crying. David said my brother was wrong to accuse me in public of killing my mother. He ordered us several cocktails as we talked until closing time. He was a considerate guy and listened to my side of the story. He took me home in his green Cadillac. We became best friends. He was a perfect gentleman, a good listener, and not judgmental. I felt safe with him.

One day, I was in the dumps, feeling real low. I was about to leave David's house to go home when he asked, "Do you want to feel better?"

I laughed. "Hell, yeah. I'm tired of feeling like shit!"

He replied, "I have something that will make the pain go away."

He had my interest as I sat back down. He went in his bedroom and came out holding a little pouch, which he called his kit. It contained a syringe, needle, small rubber tubing, spoon, and a bag of white powder.

He said, "Watch what I do." He put some white powder in the spoon and heated it with his lighter until it liquefied. He put the tubing around his arm until you could see his vein, then used the syringe to get the liquid from the spoon and shot it into his arm. He got this funny look on his face. He sighed, "Your turn."

It was ecstasy, the best feeling I'd ever experienced. I felt relaxed, calm, and sleepy. I was hooked. My life for the next ten years was a living hell because I was a drug addict. I lost everything as I lied, cheated, and stole to support my habit. I went to rehab several times, but got back on drugs.

I knew it was time to change my lifestyle when I

woke up one night lying in an alley by a dumpster with something gnawing on the toe of my boot. I've been clean three years now, but it's a struggle every day to stay drug free.

I can never forget the scars that run up and down my arms from those days. Now, when I look at my arms, they tell a story. I use cocoa butter on the scars, but it only helps a little. I usually wear long sleeves to cover my shame. Thank goodness nobody can see my toes.

The years of my addiction were horrible, but now I must let go of the past. My goal is to improve my life and reconnect with my family, which I'm doing day by day. I can't erase the damage done, but the best thing for me now is to forgive and move forward.

Tested

MR. JOHNSON, our local hero, always told the young men in the neighborhood when they complained about their jobs, "Don't quit, stick. 'Cause you gonna face these same issues anywhere you go."

They talked about discrimination; not getting the same pay as the whites, although they performed the same tasks. They'd train the white boys, who became their bosses, even though they had less experience.

One day, Mr. Johnson sat a group down and told us his story. When World War II ended in 1945, he returned home from the Navy expecting a better life. After all, they had fought for freedom and beat the bad guys. As a veteran, he thought finding work would be easier, but not for Negroes (they called us that in those days). He was turned down for all the jobs he could apply for that had potential for advancement, even though he was a high-school graduate with a year of college before being drafted. He was offered only low-paying jobs shining shoes or working as a janitor or bus boy.

Finally, he got a chance to apply for a job in one of

the big hotels in downtown Chicago to run the elevator. He did well in the interview but had one more thing to do before being hired. He had to pass the paper bag test, which they gave only to Negroes. A brown paper bag was held close to your face; if your skin tone was the same color or lighter than the bag, you got the job. Mr. Johnson was hired. He worked that job for several years until he heard that you could apply to take the exam for the post office. The post office was one of the few agencies that hired Negroes; it was a good job for us at that time.

Mr. Johnson was notified to come downtown to take the exam. The facility was crowded with men of all races and ages. The exam took several hours. You'd be contacted regarding your results within sixty days. You had to score seventy or above to be eligible for a position. Mr. Johnson received his letter stating that he scored a 93 on the test. He was excited! Now he could start making some decent money to support his family. The letter instructed him to come downtown regarding his score.

Mr. Johnson waited an hour before he was called in to discuss their issue. They wanted him to take the test again because something had to be wrong with the scoring for a Negro to rate so high. He knew then that they thought he cheated to get such a high score.

It was on a Saturday when he took the exam again. They told him to wear short sleeves, and he complied. He took the test in a room alone, except for the two white guys monitoring him. Thirty days later, he got a letter with his test results: 98. With his veteran preference, his total score was 103.

Mr. Johnson retired after forty-four years at the post office, with most of those years as a supervisor. His hard work enabled him to put two kids and a wife through college, own four apartment buildings, a gas station, and a barber's shop.

Why Me

THE FIRST TIME it happened, I was five years old. There was a family living above us on the second floor. There was a deaf girl who waved at me every morning as she stood in the window. She had a teenage brother named Albert. He was always nice to me, would give me candy and pull my braids. I got a new bike for my birthday, but my mom was too busy to show me how to ride it. Albert said he would teach me when he came home from school. I was excited.

During my first lesson, I fell, but Albert picked me up, saying it would get better. He was right. Soon I was riding my bike thanks to Albert.

One day, Albert didn't go to school. He was sitting on the stairs. He asked if I wanted to come upstairs to play with him and his sister. I was happy to go. His sister was in the front room watching cartoons; everyone else was gone. Albert grabbed my hand. He took me to the bathroom and locked the door. He put the toilet seat down, sat on it, and put me on his lap. He talked about Hi/ bike and how glad he was that I could ride. I had on a dress with matching socks. He whispered in my ear, making funny noises. I felt a sharp pain. I started to cry.

He hugged me real tight, telling me it would be all right. He told me this was our secret, not to tell anybody. He kept hugging me. He washed me up and gave me some candy. I never told anybody, but I never went upstairs again.

It wasn't long after the incident that they moved. When they left, they took my bike with them.

I was six when my mom's friend Louis started coming over frequently. They would sit in the living room talking about what they could do to make some money. Sometimes he would come over and she wouldn't be home. He would leave a message for her that he would come back later.

This one day, he came over when she was gone. He asked if he could come in and wait. I knew him, so I let him in the apartment. I was watching television. He started talking to me, but I wasn't listening to him because the cartoons were on.

All of a sudden, Louis grabbed me. He took me to the bedroom and threw me on the bed. He had a scary look in his eyes. I started crying and closed my eyes. I felt a sharp pain and hollered for my momma. He put his hand over my mouth and whispered, "Shut up or I'll kill you. You better not tell anybody. If you do, I'll find you." I kept my eyes closed the whole time.

I told my mom, but she was high on dope, so she just looked at me. She didn't say or do anything. It was in 2016, right before my aunt died that she told me: my Uncle Irvin found Louis and beat the hell out of him for what he did to me. I never knew that happened. It gave me some sense of justice after all those years.

I was seven when my mother's friend Winston would visit and give her money. He was a big guy with a brown round face with a goatee. He seemed nice. One day while visiting, he offered to take me to the movies because my mom had somewhere to go. I loved going to the movies with my cousins, so when he mentioned it, I was excited.

We got to the theater. It was a double feature. He bought me popcorn, gummy bears, and a drink. I was sitting in my seat when he picked me up and sat me on his lap, saying this way I could see better. As I was watching the movie, he started rubbing on me. A little later, he put his hand inside my panties as he mumbled to himself.

I tried to move, but he held me tight. I dropped my popcorn. Afterwards he took me home. The next time he came to take me to the movies, I cried that I didn't want to go. I hid under the bed until he left. It was years later when I was sitting in the kitchen talking to my Aunt Constance, when she told me that she saw Winston and he asked about me.

I said, "You tell that pervert to go to hell!" My aunt looked at me in amazement!

My Aunt Bette needed a babysitter for her three girls for the summer. Her regular babysitter had surgery, unable to work for several months. She said she would pay me, and I could spend the summer with my cousins. I was glad to do it. My aunt lived on 39th and Lake Park, which was in walking distance to the beach. It was fun to spend time with my aunt because she'd take us bowling and to the movies. When she got home from work, I had some free time. I would walk over to the beach.

This particular day, a boy who lived in the same building as my aunt stopped me as I was walking across the bridge. He asked where I was going. I said, "To the beach." He said he wanted to get to know me better and asked if we could talk for a few minutes. He said I was cute. I thought he was cute too. I was thirteen, he was seventeen. He was friendly, seemed nice.

After an hour, I told him it was time for me to leave so I could go to the beach and get back home before dark. All of a sudden, he grabbed me by the collar.

He said, "You ain't going nowhere."

I told him to let me go and pushed him.

There was none around but us. He grabbed me again by my throat.

He said, "You're gonna give me some pussy or I'll choke you to death." I was terrified.

He took me under the bridge in the bushes and raped me. Afterwards, he said if I told anybody, he'd kill me. I was so ashamed. I never told my aunt.

I stopped going to the beach and stayed in the apartment. I saw him one time after the ordeal. He came up to me, took my transistor radio, winked at me, and walked away. I made sure to avoid him for the rest of the summer. I was glad to get back home to Morgan Park. I never told my grandma either.

Impressions

Also by Zenobia Orimoloye

Bits of Pieces: Sixteen Poem and Four Short Stories

Choices: Thirteen Short Stories

Reflections: Short Stories of Memorable Moments

Passages: Up Close and Personal Short Stories

Family

Every two years, we have a family reunion. Relatives come from all over the country since its the only time some of us get to see one another. This is the last time I'm going to organize it. It's time to rotate the responsibility 'cause it's a lot of work. It's sad that some of us live in the same city, only socializing when there's a reunion. Everyone's busy with their lives, trying to make a living in these challenging times. It tests your nerves trying to get relatives to pay their fees to cover the food, the picnic, the dance, activities for the kids, and hotel reservations. Some pay right away. Others, you have to hound them like a bill collector.

Once the time arrives, it's great to see sisters, brothers, uncles, grandparents, cousins, and family friends. You get a chance to catch up on the family gossip.

Some family members you like better than others—that's when tolerance is put to the test. We can be civil to each other during this time. It's a delight to connect with your relatives. I have a first cousin, Kevin Moore, a.k.a. "Bones" 'cause he was always skinny, even as a child. He's tall and thin, with a gift for gab.

In our family, you get a nickname at birth that sticks

with you for the rest of your life. Bones and I live in the same city but only see each other at the reunion. He usually finds me and hugs me tightly for about a minute, giving me a wink as he walks away. That's our interaction during the entire reunion. Although we never talk, we have a close connection because we've shared a secret since childhood.

Bones' mother, Aunt Flo, got pregnant with him when she was a teenager. The father was a guy named Richard, who was killed when Bones was a baby. I heard family members talk about Richard: *Richard wasn't wrapped too tight. I don't know why Flo got mixed up with him. Lord, I hope it don't pass down to Bones.*

I asked my dad what "not wrapped too tight" meant. He said, "It's someone who acts odd, like talking to themselves while walking down the street looking up at the sky." I was satisfied with the explanation, not thinking anything about it until the incident. I heard Bones shouting at one of the boys on our block who teased, "Bones, you crazy like your daddy."

Bones jumped off his bike and hit the boy in the mouth. He cried, "Say it again, and I'll stomp you in the ground. I ain't crazy, dammit, I'm not." Bones had tears in his eyes. I felt sorry for him.

People in the neighborhood knew not to call Bones crazy cause he'd beat the shit out of you. Bones had a temper. If you made him mad, your ass was grass, and he was the lawnmower. Bones protected me too. I was an only child, so he was like a big brother to me. He was twelve and I was ten. If someone bothered me, once they knew Bones was my cousin, they left me alone. Bones was our grandmother's favorite—he could do no wrong. She wouldn't believe you anyway, if you said her boy did something bad. We were taught that family sticks together.

Aunt Flo lived on the third floor of a big red brick building. There was a back porch with a long bannister that all the kids liked to sit on. We'd lean back, pretending to fall. We thought it was fun, but the grown folks constantly told us not to play on the bannister 'cause it was dangerous. We didn't listen and kept doing it.

Every Sunday, we had dinner over at a relative's house. It was Aunt Flo's turn to host it. I loved desserts, usually sweet potato pie and peach cobbler—my favorites. This Sunday, Aunt Flo invited her friend Carmen and Carmen's daughter Gloria over for dinner. Bones was there watching football when they arrived. I was in the kitchen chopping onions and celery for the cornbread dressing.

Gloria took a liking to Bones, following him around and pulling on his curly hair. He would smile at her and wink. I could tell she was getting on his nerves, so I called her to come help me in the kitchen. She came in there for a little while but was bored, not interested in chopping anything. I didn't want to do it either, but my mom made me.

Bones was on the back porch leaning over the bannister talking to someone walking down the alley. A few minutes later, I looked out on the porch. There was Gloria sitting on the bannister smiling in Bones' face. He was sick of her now.

He said, "Leave me alone. Take your ugly ass in the house."

Gloria snickered, "Who you calling ugly. At least my daddy wasn't crazy. I bet you crazy like him." She pointed her finger in his face, laughing. Bones pushed her over the bannister.

I was standing in the kitchen when Bones ran past me

for help. Everybody ran from the living room to the porch. They asked Bones, "What happened?" He explained that Gloria was playing on the bannister and he told her to stop, but she leaned back too far and he couldn't catch her. Bones had tears in his eyes.

Gloria's mother screamed as she leaned over the bannister. "Oh lord, my baby's dead." She cried and cried. The ambulance came, along with the police. Bones repeated his story to the officers, who noted it as a terrible accident with a kid playing on the bannister.

It was a horrible Sunday. That evening before I left, Bones hugged me, nodded his head, and gave me a wink. We never discussed it. After all, family must stick together.

Hollywood

I could hear the sisters crying in JI the background as I gave the sad news to Irene's husband about Sylvia. She died the night before from breast cancer. Sylvia was the oldest sister who lived in Baldwin Hills, but the family always told people she lived in Hollywood. She moved there in the 1940s to seek a better life, maybe get in the movies like Hattie McDaniel, who won an Academy Award for best supporting actress in *Gone with the Wind.*

She could play maid roles, too. Sylvia resembled a movie star from that time named Dorothy Lamour. Sylvia was the color of butter, with thick wavy hair that she wore in a braid down her back. There were four sisters—Irene, Darlene, Rosetta, and Sylvia. It was hard times back then, but more difficult for Negroes to find work that paid a living wage.

There were rumors about Sylvia, like she was a mistress for a rich white man, involved with gangsters, or she was passing as white. It didn't matter what people said about Sylvia because her sisters adored her. She kept the family together, sending money for food and rent. The sisters lived together to share expenses. They were in their sixties. Sylvia was seventy-five at the time of her death.

Even when they married, Sylvia was still head of the family, even though she lived thousands of miles away. The main reason they depended on her was because Sylvia was the smartest, and she had money. When Darlene's son Ray Ray was jailed for raping a white girl, Sylvia paid for the best Chicago attorney, who got Ray Ray out of jail. The case was thrown out for insufficient evidence.

When Irene's husband needed $20,000 to buy a liquor store, Sylvia sent the money as a gift. Sylvia paid for Rosetta's son to become a doctor. She was always there for her family. Sylvia never married or had children.

Now let me tell you how Sylvia made her money in Hollywood. She didn't get in the movies. She'd audition for parts but was told she wasn't black enough. They wanted an Aunt Jemima type. She got desperate for work, so she applied at an agency that hired domestics. She was a maid for one family but quit because the father, son, and mother kept trying to bed her. Hollywood was something else.

A friend of Sylvias had an interview for a maid job, but got sick, allowing Sylvia to go in her place. She was interviewed by a famous Hollywood star, who hired her on the spot because she liked Sylvia's face and hands. Sylvia wouldn't tell her real name, but she always called her Kate. Sylvia became her maid, companion, and confidant.

Kate was bisexual and had to be very careful because of her career. Sylvia lived in an apartment over the garage. Kate taught Sylvia how to drive, so she could chauffeur her around town. Sylvia travelled with Kate all over the world. She coordinated wild Hollywood parties for Kate and her friends. Sylvia hired her friends to help and paid them well to keep their mouths shut; it was good money for them. They didn't pay the Colored any mind at the parties; they were just the help. Sylvia would tell me about those parties—men with men, women with women, threesomes, orgies, and sometimes dogs were involved. One time, a well-known actress sprayed some whip cream on her coochie, letting the dog lick it off. Sylvia's discretion solidified her relationship with Kate, and they became lifelong friends.

Kate invested money for Sylvia and bought her some Disney stock. Whenever Sylvia needed money, she'd just go to the safe and get the money, leaving an IOU. Sylvia worked for Kate for twenty-five years, even after she retired from the movie business. Kate, who was a heavy smoker, contracted lung cancer. Sylvia cared for her until the end. Kate never married or had children. Six months before her death; Kate destroyed all Sylvias IOUs and gave Sylvia the Disney stock she'd bought for her years ago. After her death, Kate's will left the bulk of her estate to the Motion Picture and Television Country House and Hospital in Woodland Hills, Los Angeles, and a million dollars for Sylvia.

Sylvia remained in California, opening a beauty shop, along with buying a boarding house for rental income. She enjoyed the warm weather and had no desire to return to Chicago. A tabloid contacted Sylvia, willing to pay her good money to tell about her life with Kate. But Sylvia refused, loyal friend to the end.

She'd visit her family twice a year. Two months before her death, Sylvia completed her will, leaving each sister $500,000, and me, Jarvis Mills, her companion for twenty years, her house and the Disney stock. Sylvia did well for herself in Hollywood.

Justice

A year ago, my son Patrick was gunned down due to his refusal to join a gang. The shootings in Chicago make national news frequently, even though other cities are just as bad.

You never get over the death of a child. I have an ache in me that won't go away. Smokey's the low life who killed Patrick, although the police couldn't get anyone to come forward. My neighbor's son, Ronnie, age ten, saw the shooting but was afraid to tell the police. There's a saying: "Snitches end up in ditches." Since people won't speak up, the violence will continue.

Smokey's been a gang member since age twelve, dropping out of high school to run with gangs, a smart kid with a B+ average who felt school was a waste of time. She's called Smokey 'cause she likes getting high, been doing it since she was ten. She runs with the guys because she proved she was fearless by turning into a cold-blooded killer.

She gets the upper hand because girls aren't viewed as killers. She's terrorized the neighborhood for years. She's nineteen now, an enforcer for her gang. I heard she likes her work. Her signature is three shots to the head to make sure you're dead. She's known for burning down a store if the owner won't pay for protection, or killing people targeted by her gang. I see her walking around smoking weed, trying to recruit new gang members by flashing money and giving out Jordans. She thinks she's tough, killing unarmed boys for sport. I despise her!

I plan on moving out of this area this year. My ten-year-old daughter Nia needs to get out of this environment before it swallows her up. I don't want that scum trying to recruit her to be a ho for the gang members. I want a better life for Nia.

I guess Smokey can't help it, since her parents are gang members, with her father in jail for drug dealing. She has two younger brothers she's prepping to follow in her footsteps. Whenever the police question Smokey, her mother always gives her an alibi, and with no witnesses, they can't arrest her. Last weekend, thirty people were shot and ten died. I heard that Smokey killed five of the people who were selling drugs in her territory. She's violent as hell. I'll admit, she scares me too.

Two years ago, the city tore down the projects in the inner city, due to gentrification. They gave the residents Section 8 vouchers to move anywhere that would accept them. Some moved out of state; others moved further south to areas like ours.

We had an influx of new gang-bangers in the area who posed a threat to the gangs already here. The shootings increased as the gangs competed for drug territory and who would control it. It was hell! People were whispering, "Smokey got promoted in the organization. She's running with the big dogs. She's got a new Corvette, her own apartment, nice clothes, and plenty of cash. She's moving up fast."

It was a Saturday evening around 7 p.m. Smokey was sitting in her red Corvette, talking on the phone. I could see her from my second-floor apartment. All of a sudden, a black SUV pulled up beside her with guns blasting. Smokey tried to get to her gun, but it was too late. She stumbled out of her car and fell to the ground, twitching, with blood spurting out of her mouth. Her white shirt was soaked with blood. I waited until all movement stopped, then I called 911.

Last Hurrah

We're in our seventies now. Craig and I have been married forty years. I met him on a blind date. He was a Vietnam vet, and I usually left those guys alone.

His goodnight kiss made me dizzy, so I had to see him again. We've had our problems over the years, but we worked them out together. He was unfaithful in his younger days, which led me to have an affair during one of our separations. 1 left him twice, going back to him when he pleaded on his knees, "Baby, I love you, need you, can't live without you. Give me one more chance. I'll make it up to you. Please, please, please come back."

Our kids are grown, living in different parts of the country—Milwaukee, Houston, and Atlanta. Of course, we see our son and his family often because they're closer, living in Milwaukee. Over the years, we've settled into a comfortable life growing old and grey together.

Craig was an excellent lover, very affectionate. He's an awesome kisser, which was great foreplay. We had an active sex life for years. During our thirties, forties, and fifties, it was two to three times a day. In our sixties, it slowed to twice a week, which was still good, considering some of our friends' sex life ended years ago. We love slow-dancing, since it always got us in the mood.

Finally, our sexual relations stopped in our seventies. Craigs seventy-two, and I'm seventy-four. He says, "Pearl, weve had a good run, but all good things must come to an end."

Craig has diabetes, high blood pressure, and a bad back. I have high blood pressure, underactive thyroid, and bad hips. We accept our limitations and think about the good old days when we were limber and in good shape, with lots of energy. Growing old is not so bad considering the alternative. The golden years are good for me 'cause Craig's a companion I like and love.

It was a Friday morning when UPS dropped off a brown box for Craig on the front porch. I thought it was a present for me. He was always surprising me with gifts. I got the box and took it upstairs to Craig, who was still in bed. I gave him the box. His eyes lit up. He exclaimed, "Baby, we're going to have some fun this weekend. The VA doctor recommended this item for my condition."

I hadn't seen him this excited in a while. He opened the box, which had items in different shapes, sizes, and colors. Craig put on his glasses as he touched the items in the box. I just stared at him, perplexed.

He read aloud, "Please read the entire manual and watch the DVD before using this system." I picked up the VA user guide for Osbon ErecAid Esteem Vacuum Therapy System. I read, "The ErecAid Esteem system is intended to artificially produce an erection in males suffering from erectile dysfunction (impotence) in order to facilitate sexual intercourse or to create and maintain erections by providing oxygen-rich blood flow to the penis."

What the hell! Craig chuckled. "Baby, you want to give it a try?" I wanted to say no, but the look in his eyes showed me he wanted this for us. I replied with a fake smile. "Sure, luv, no problem." I thought that stuff looked like a small vacuum cleaner with attachments. We spent the day working on the damn thing.

We had to check to make sure the following components were included in the box (one each):

Multilingual DVD (English, Francais, Espanol, Nederlands, and Deutsch)

- Component Order Form
- Osbon Personal Lubricant
- Inverse Tapered Clear Cylinder with Insert
- Erect Aid Esteem Manual Pump Handle
- Easy Action Ring Loader
- .750 Pink Medium "D" High Tension Ring
- .750 Beige Medium "C" Standard Tension Ring
- .875 Beige Large "A" Standard Tension Ring

At this point, I had no interest in this thing; but Craig was determined to put it together. There were many pictures and diagrams on how to put this contraption on the penis. We tried to assemble the pump, cylinder; and insert. I suggested that we sit down, read the manual and watch the DVD as instructed.

We spent all day and evening trying to put it together. My neck was hurting; Craig's penis was raw from pulling on it, as we tried to get the proper fit for using the ring tension. He was expected to do practice sessions for at least ten to fifteen minutes daily for a minimum of two weeks. Hell: we were exhausted already, and still couldn't assemble it correctly to get it to work.

Craig mumbled; "This is too much." We put the parts back in the box and threw it in the trash. It was 10 p.m. that night when we drank some cold beers while watching our favorite DVD, Black Bootyland, which led to some heavy petting. The next morning, we were spooning in bed when Craig whispered, "We'll never have intercourse again. My penis just won't work anymore."

I chuckled while rubbing his bald head. "You're still the best kisser in the world. That's enough for me, luv."

Law & Order

SHOTS RANG OUT in the night as a body fell to the ground. The shooters could report back to the gang that the snitch was dead. As they drove off, they saw the guy limping down the street. They drove back around to finish him off when they realized he'd stumbled into the 22nd District.

They backed up quickly and drove off. On the way back, the driver told his cohort what he would say to the gang. "Everybody knows you don't fuck around with the 22nd District 'cause Captain Ed Jones don't play. He's a Chicago hero; especially on the Southside, since he brought those fifty brothers back from human traffickers. He made front page news. His officers are called the 'Blood Hounds' 'cause they'll hunt you down until they get you. We'll get that snitch another time."

Captain Jones arrived at the station at 8:30 a.m. sharp. He's fifty years old, looking forty in top shape with mingled grey hair. He's six-feet-three-inches tall, a widower with two grown sons. The older son's married, living in Evanston, Illinois. The youngest one lives with him in their home in Beverly, one of the upscale neighborhoods in Chicago. He graduated from Howard

University with a master's degree in criminal justice.

Today's a special day for the captain because tonight at 6 p.m. at the Palmer House, he's being honored by his commander for the excellent work he's done. The Morgan Park 22nd District stats are looking good, and crime is down in the area.

That night, Captain Jones was brought on stage with a standing ovation as his commander shook his hand and gave him a commendation for his district. Captain Jones thanked his officers and staff and got off the stage. A few deals were made that night. Two of Jones' officers were selected to attend specialized training for two weeks. He was pleased to see Black officers getting this opportunity. He's also getting two employees, an IT specialist and Zora Khan, an officer who'd been ostracized by her colleagues.

The commander told Jones, "I'm retiring soon and recommended you as an outstanding candidate for my job. It's been a pleasure working with you over the years." Captain Jones was honored that his commander thought so highly of him. The commander continued, "Enough work talk. Let's eat, drink, and make merry."

On Monday morning, Officer Zora Khan reported for duty. She was nervous as she sat down in Captain Jones's office. Zora was average height with her hair pulled back in a bun. He said, "Welcome, Officer Khan, to the 22nd District. I want you to do me a favor. I want you to share your story during roll call, and it'll never be mentioned again.

Zora replied, "I really don't like talking about it, but I'll do it."

Captain Jones introduced Zora at roll call, telling his officers he requested that she share some information with them. Zora said, "Most of you have heard rumors about me, so here's the story: It was an ordinary day as we were driving near Washington Park on 51st Street. My partner spotted a young Black man who favored a suspect that had been involved in a series of robberies in the area. We followed him for a bit as he was walking down the street. We pulled up close to him, requesting that he stop so we could talk to him. He ignored us. We called out again for him to stop.

He didn't stop, so we chased him. You know we get mad when we have to chase a suspect. By this time, a second squad car pulled up. The suspect tripped and fell to the ground. The two male officers got to him before me, one white and the other Hispanic. They were stomping him in his genitals. I asked them to stop, but t they wouldn't t, so I pulled them away from the suspect because a crowd had gathered to watch the abuse.

The suspect was lying on the ground, screaming in pain. The officers were offended that I didn't side with them. I don't care—wrong is wrong. There was no need to treat him that way.

After checking, it was discovered that he had no criminal record and was not the robbery guy. The family filed a lawsuit. I had to testify, told the truth, refused to lie. The family won their case. I was black balled; my life was threatened. Officers refused to work with me. They felt I couldn't be trusted. I was given an office job to protect me. I'm not ashamed of my actions. That's all I've got to say."

There was total silence until someone in the back said, "Based on your confession, you must bring the donuts tomorrow."

This broke the ice; there was laughter all around, except for two officers who weren't smiling.

Captain Jones added, "I'll assign Zora a partner within forty-eight hours. If you have a problem working with her, come talk to me about it. Okay, everyone, let's get to work."

Only two officers expressed concerns about working with Zora, who was assigned to work with Officer John Abimbola, a five-year veteran with several commendations. He was ambitious, eager to make detective, and had no intention of refusing the assignment. He had enormous respect for the captain, his mentor and role model.

John was tall, a workaholic, and a health nut, fond of protein shakes and daily workouts. He met Zora in the interrogation room to talk before they went out on the street. His advice to her: "Pay attention, listen, don't make the same mistake twice, and we'll get along fine. Now let's get to the squad car. I'm driving."

The first week was uneventful, as they drove through the neighborhoods and down the alleys. They'd stop the car, speak to people at the fast-food places, gas stations, and parks. They bought lunch at the health food store. John got a veggie sandwich with a protein shake and plantain chips. Zora got a turkey burger with a salad.

While eating in the car, they chatted. John divulged that he was the black sheep of his family because he didn't become a doctor, lawyer, or engineer. Those were the careers that mattered to his father, who was Nigerian; his mother was Black American. His parents met in college. His father was a mechanical engineer, and his mother was an attorney. They retired and moved to Arizona for the winter months. John's brother was an emergency room doctor, married to a nurse, with two sons.

"I was supposed to go to law school after graduating

from Northwestern University, but decided to become a police officer," John said. "My parents were very disappointed, but they gradually accepted my career choice. Anyway, my brother is my savior because he did all the right things." John admitted that at thirty years old, he still lived at home with his parents.

Zora shared that she was divorced from a Muslim guy who wanted four sons and an obedient wife who did what she was told. After five years of marriage, she got out. She graduated from Loyola University with an accounting degree. She worked two boring years at an accounting firm and shares a townhouse with her older sister, who works at the Social Security Administration, along with her mother, as a claims authorizes Her father owns a funeral home with his brother. Zora applied for jobs with the Internal Revenue Service, which is a good agency to work for since they bring in the money and they offer an excellent training program for agents.

John chuckled. "Now that we've spilled our guts, let's get back to work, partner." As they were driving down 115th Street, they saw a black Chrysler 300 run a red light. John turned on the siren and pursued the driver. The car stopped, and two guys jumped out, running.

Zora jumped out of the car, chasing the one with the white hoodie, while John drove around looking for the one in the red shirt. Zora caught her man, wrestled him down, and cuffed him. John tracked the other one as he ran down a dead-end alley. The car was stolen. By the time they booked the two men and completed the paperwork, their shift was over.

The weeks went by, and they settled into a routine. They drove through the neighborhoods, waving at kids. They parked in front of the liquor store to talk to some of the guys standing on the corner. John and Zora hung together after work, too, joining the Sunday afternoon police bowling team. Zora was elated that most of her colleagues accepted her, except for the two who glared at her, but she decided to ignore them. She was grateful that Captain Jones gave her the opportunity for a fresh start. She wouldn't let him down. And she enjoyed working with John—he treated her as an equal.

John and Zora worked well in emergency situations by being decisive and taking appropriate action. Statistically, they were making the district look better. They arrested suspects with no complaints of abuse. They diffused several domestic violence issues by talking to the culprits and persuading them to take anger management classes and go to AA meetings in lieu of jail. They checked on them weekly. They had a good reputation in the neighborhood. John stopped a man with a baby from jumping off a five-story building. Zora rescued two children from a burning building. They were dubbed "The Caped Crusaders" by their fellow officers, who constantly teased them.

Captain Jones decided to temporarily assign Zora and John to the detective unit since several of them had recently retired. It was a month later that the captain called them into the office to discuss an assignment. He spoke to them candidly, "There's a serial rapist running rampant on the Southside of Chicago raping Black women. It's not mentioned on the TV stations or re ported in the local newspapers. Now he's doing it in my district. This has been happening for several months, and I want him caught. You two have been getting results. You caught the dollar-store robbers using a dropped lottery ticket, along with marked money from a bored store clerk who wrote her initials on the back of the money. You also solved a car-jacking ring by manipulating one of the car-jackers to turn on his buddy and give solid evidence against their ringleader that led to his arrest. I'm assigning you this case. Go out there and do what you do. I'm counting on you two."

John grunted as they returned to their desks to discuss a plan of action. "Hell, Zora, rape cases are tough. The victims usually don't want to testify, or they feel ashamed and won't cooperate."

Zora responded, "I volunteered two years with Chicago Women Against Rape. I'll check with them to see what information they can give me. Come on, let's get started. I want to interview some of the rape victims to see what they can remember."

Two weeks later, another woman was raped in the 22nd District. Zora and John arrived at the scene before the ambulance. The girl was moaning, calling for her mama. Zora held her hand until the ambulance came, taking her to the nearest hospital. The crime scene unit came in to secure the site and gather what evidence they could find.

By the time John and Zora arrived at the hospital, the victim, Kim Perry, was asleep. Rape procedures were followed, but she was sedated due to a panic attack. Her mother was on her way. John and Zora were told to come back in the morning to get a statement from the victim.

The next morning, they talked to Kim. She explained, "I'm twenty-one years old, working at a nursing home to save money to buy a car. Usually I get a ride, but the person was sick. It was about 9 p.m. I had gotten off the bus, walking the three blocks to my house. As I crossed by the alley, a figure out of nowhere grabbed me and dragged me into the alley. As I screamed for help, I bit him. He punched me twice in the face, tore off my skirt and panties, and raped me. It was over in a matter of seconds. He spit on me before he ran away. His eyes were red and scary. He had a face mask on. You could only see his eyes and mouth. I stumbled out to the street. A man saw me and called the police. That's it."

Kim's face was swollen with two black eyes. She was thoroughly examined, with all evidence secured and tagged. John left to write the report. Zora stayed a little longer to console Kim, hoping she might remember something about the rapist. Zora held her hand whispering, "I understand. I'm a rape survivor. I promise you we'll catch him. Our captain made your case top priority. You get your rest and get some counseling. Talk to the hospital social worker for a referral." The hunt began. John and Zora talked to people in the area, asking if they heard anything. They interviewed other rape victims who were hostile or didn't want to talk about it. One snickered, "Nobody cares about Black women being raped. They think we a bunch of hos and bitches getting what we deserve." Another victim said, "He was a musty motherfucker with stanky breath. Thank God he had a little dick 'cause I didn't feel a thing. It was over in a few seconds. You couldn't see his face with that black mask on."

Two weeks later, no leads. John was checking his inbox at the station when he saw two phone messages from Greenwood over at the Crime Scene Unit. John told Zora, "My buddy Greenwood left me two messages. Let's go see what he wants. I'm tired of sitting around here."

They grabbed their jackets and rushed out to the squad car. Greenwood was out for lunch, so they waited for him. Fifteen minutes later, Greenwood walked in drinking a Diet Coke. Joe Greenwood was glad to see his old buddy, John. Joe said, "Congrats on getting that detective assignment. I see Captain Jones is grooming you. He's a good guy, made us proud bringing those guys back. He cares about his people. He's righteous. I heard he's up for a promotion to commander. Hope he gets it."

John sighed, "Man, we're working on a serial rapist case with no leads. No identification 'cause he wore a black mask." Greenwood responded, "I called you to give the results of the evidence found at the crime scene. There was blood on the victim's blouse. We assumed it was hers and took samples for analyzing. But there was another blood type besides hers. She's O positive. The other sample's AB negative, which isn't common. I was checking for STDs when I noticed something interesting."

John and Zora look puzzled.

Greenwood continued, "Sickle cell anemia is a condition when there's not enough healthy blood cells to carry adequate oxygen throughout your body. Normally, your red blood cells are flexible and round, moving easily through your blood vessels. In sickle cell anemia, the red blood cells become rigid and sticky and are shaped like sickles. This disease is very painful. Most people with sickle cell are of African descent, which is us. The guy with this disease probably takes medication to reduce the painful attacks and the need for blood transfusions. I did some digging. The drug usually prescribed for this disease is Hydroxyurea. That's all I got for you now."

Zora was excited. She grabbed Greenwood and gave him a great big hug. John stood there staring at her as she grabbed his arm and ushered him out to discuss her idea in the car.

She said, "It may sound crazy, but hear me out. Now we know there's a Black male with sickle cell disease who can barely complete the act. Let's check to see who's using Hydroxyurea in our district. It'll take a lot of phone calls to Walgreens, CVS, and Walmart to check for who has the disease and who's using that medicine. I'll work on my own time."

Johns responded, "Okay, let's give it a try. We have nothing to lose."

After three days calling pharmacies, nothing. They were busy or wouldn't return their calls. This case was going nowhere.

On Monday morning, Zora dropped her muffin as she answered the phone. She was grumpy as she picked up the receiver. As she listened, her eyes got big, and she continued to nod her head. John was watching her intently.

Zora hung up the phone and grabbed her coat, shouting, "Let's go! I'll share it with you as you're driving. The pharmacy tech on the phone just saw our message. She had been on leave for two days. A Black guy named Shawn Morris at 11416 S. Aberdeen came in yesterday to purchase the Hydroxyurea for his sickle cell disease. Let's go get the video to get a look at him."

Back at the station, they briefed Captain Jones about the case. He cautioned: "Follow proper procedures and build a strong case that'll hold up in court. Make sure you got the right guy. I'm behind your 100 percent. Get that bastard!"

Shawn Morris didn't have a police record. He was a clean-cut, average-looking guy, no tattoos. John and Zora watched his house for a couple hours a day to monitor his activities. He left around 9 a.m. to catch the 9:30 a.m. bus. They assumed he was going to work, since this was his routine for three days. John and Zora decided to pick him up on Friday at 8:30 a.m.

Thursday evening, after work, Zora stopped by the

last victim, Kim Perrys house, to check on her. Kim's face looked better. She was receiving rape counseling and took some time off work. She lived with her mom, along with two sisters. Zora talked with Kim for a while, leaving her business card with her in case she remembered anything.

Friday morning, John and Zora drove to Shawn Morriss residence and rang the bell. A grey-haired lady opened the door. Zora and John identified themselves as police detectives, looking for Shawn Morris.

The woman asked, "Why do you want to talk to my grandson?"

John responded, "He may be able to assist us in an investigation we're conducting."

The woman yelled, "Shawn, the police want to see you." Shawn came to the door dressed in sweat. John explained, you need to come down to the station now for questioning in a rape case. Bring your ID with you please."

Shawn asked, "For what? Did someone identify me?" He stared at John for a minute, never looking at Zora. He agreed to go with them. He told his grandma, "This is all a misunderstanding. They got the wrong guy. You know we all look alike. Call my job, tell them I won't be in today. I'll see them on Monday."

He rode with the officers to the station. Shawn was cool, calm, and cocky. He was soft-spoken. He was put in the interrogation room, read his rights, and offered to have an attorney provided to him. He chuckled, "I don't need an attorney cause I'm innocent. You barking up the wrong tree."

Zora explained, "Were working on a case dealing with a rapist with the sickle cell disease. It was brought to our attention that you had it and bought Hydroxyurea.

His reply, "Come on now, I'm sure there's other people with sickle cell disease buying this medicine. What else you got? Can anybody identify this rapist? I'm twentyfive years old with no arrest record." He leaned back in the chair with his arms folded across his chest, grinning. At this time, Zora got an urgent call. John was left in the room with Shawn, but John decided to wait until Zora came back to resume the interrogation. She returned fifteen minutes later, and the questioning continued.

Shawn yawned, "This is harassment. Can I go home now, officers?" Zora leaned over the table and stared him in the face, as she murmured, "I'm so sorry about your deformity. Shawn, you only have one ball. What happened to the other one? Is that why your penis is so small? His whole face changed. He snarled, you fucking cunt. I hate you stuck-up Black bitches with your loud vulgar asses. Judging a man by his dick size? Yeah, I raped them. They weren't so smug then because I had the power." He lunged across the table, hitting Zora in the face. John grabbed him, threw him on the floor, and cuffed him. Shawn shouted, "I want a lawyer, goddammit. I want a lawyer now!" Shawn was booked and taken to lockup.

John was surprised that Zora came up with that bit of information. She explained, "The call was from Kim Perry. I stopped by her house last night and left my card, telling her to call me if she remembered anything about the rapist. She thought he only had one ball because when she was trying to stop him from entering her, she only felt one."

Shawn Morris was dubbed "The Deformed Rapist" on the evening news and in the newspapers. It was on TV all day. Captain Jones gave an excellent press conference praising his officers for their hard work. John and Zora were standing next to him.

The next day, when Zora and John came into the office, there was a cake with the inscription "Congrats Caped Crusaders." Everyone was clapping and feeling good. The 22nd District wins again.

Captain Jones called John and Zora into his office. He was grinning from ear to ear like a proud papa.

He chortled, "I'm so proud of you two. You did an awesome job. You'll be appointed permanent detectives. You'll get commendations for solving this case. Hey, Caped Crusaders, let's go eat some cake!"

Missing

I don't want you to think ill of me because what happened wasn't my fault. My next-door neighbors were Ruby Andrews and her husband Leon. They were nice enough; but sometimes their arguments were a little too loud for me.

Ruby constantly berated Leon whenever I went out on the front porch to smoke. She got worse after he lost his job at the paint company after working there fifteen years. His unemployment ended with no job in sight.

Leon's sixty years old, needing two more years before he qualifies for Social Security. Ruby resented Leon because she was still working while he was at home every day not contributing financially.

Every time I was on the porch smoking, she would come out to complain about him. She smirked, "I guess he thinks he's too good to work at fast-food places like McDonald's^ Burger King, or Amazon. Those places are paying fifteen dollars an hour nowadays. He keeps saying he has a bad back and can't stand on his feet all day."

I told her, "You've been with Leon fifteen years. He's always worked, except for this past year when he was laid off. It's difficult for a man his age to find work. Once he gets his Social Security, you'll have additional income." She retorted, "That's two years from now. He'd better do something, or I'll divorce him."

I waved goodbye and went back into the house. They had a big fight that night. I heard screaming, along with some cuss words. Leon shouted, "Get off my back, you black snake bitch."

Ruby screamed, "Motherfucker, who you think you talking to, some ho in the street? You better bring some money in this house or get your ass out. I'm paying all the bills around here. In a big city like Chicago, you can find some kind of work. I don't care if you have to shovel shit. Get a job, asshole."

I heard the back door slam and someone running down the steps. I guess Leon left before they got physical.

It was a month later when I heard them having another fight. Ruby shouted, "Don't you touch me. I'll blow your head off. Don't make me shoot you. Get your fucking ass out. Don't come back unless you got some money in your pocket."

I heard someone running down the back steps. An hour later, I went to the store to get some cigarettes. As I was driving, I saw Leon sitting on the bench in the park. I stopped and waved for him to come get in the car. He looked pitiful as he sat in the car with his head hanging down. I drove back home, parked the car in my garage in the back, and invited him in for a drink. He came in, sitting at the kitchen table looking like he'd lost his last friend. I told him he could sleep in the basement since it had a bathroom and sofa bed down there. I figured Ruby would calm down by morning, then he could go home.

The next day, which I'll never forget, was March 17, 2020. ABC Morning News reported that the coronavirus, which began in Wuhan, China, had spread to touch nearly every corner of the globe. Hundreds of thousands of people around the world became sickened and thousands of others died. The President shut down the USA. Thank God I'm retired with a pension. What the hell's going on?

Leon was still asleep in the morning. I woke him up, turned on the TV in the basement, and we watched the news in amazement. My daughter called from Houston, and my son called from Atlanta. I told Leon to call Ruby, apologize, and go back home.

He sighed, "I just want some respect. Can't find work. I'm sick of fighting with Ruby. I just want some peace. I'll call her in a few days." I went upstairs to fix breakfast—bacon, eggs, and grits with toast.

The next day I was on the porch smoking when Ruby came out. She chuckled, "Thank goodness I'm essential, since I work at a hospital. We had a meeting yesterday about the virus. We're going to be working at lot of overtime. I put Leon out the other night, but he'll come back once relatives or friends get tired of him mooching off them. My kids never accepted Leon as a stepdad; they're grown now. They thought I could've done better than his dumb country ass. Of course, they didn't like their daddy either." I just looked at her and smiled as I went back into the house. Leon heard everything she said and went back down into the basement.

It's been a month now with the virus raging on. Leon and I are enjoying our shelter-in-place time together. Every time he thinks about going back, he'll hear her say some negative shit about him. We have a routine. We watch the morning news, exercise for thirty minutes, eat breakfast, watch The View—'cause Leon's a big fan of Whoopi Goldberg.

Every morning, I go out to take a smoke and talk with Ruby. She says she thought about calling the police to report him missing, but her kids said look at it as a blessing that the loser's gone. I asked her, "Do you miss him? Did you call his family or friends?"

She said, "I ain't got time to track him down. I'm making this money. My paychecks are looking mighty good. He'll bring his old, broke ass home eventually."

I replied, "You probably right," as I rushed to answer the phone.

It's been four months now. Leon and I hunkered down due to the virus. I stopped smoking, so I don't go on the porch that often. Anyway, Ruby's working a lot of hours due to overtime, so she's seldom home.

I go shopping once a week for the items we need. I must admit, we're having a good time. I signed up for cable, selecting Showtime, HBO, and Netflix, which allows us to view a variety of shows. I should feel guilty, but I don't. I've been without sex for twelve years, so I was stunned one night when Leon slid his hand under my robe. I opened my legs wide so he could easily get to the spot. Yessss, those magical fingers! It was a sight to behold, two old farts having sex.

I pushed him up against the wall, grinding on his privates. His eyes got big when I got the whip cream out of the fridge. All those years with no sex, I had Leon panting, moaning, calling my name. "Oh Hattie, Hattie, don't stop!"

Well, I had to hurry 'cause my leg got a cramp. One time, there was no whip cream, so I improvised with orange juice and Saran Wrap. I must say, Leon is very limber for an old dude, gives a great lap dance, and has the longest tongue I've ever seen.

Don't think badly of me. But if you do, I don't care 'cause I'm having the time of my life!

Temptation

I WAS GIDDY TODAY, since it was time to take my trip. I've been looking forward to it all week, ensuring that everything would go smoothly. I got my itinerary for the journey, and I drove off in the car.

My venture took me to the grocery store, credit union, post office, and Walgreens. What a day. This is my life since COVID-19 hit the country. It's the little things that fill your day—texting, talking on the phone, reading, going to the mailbox, playing games, and taking historical quizzes on the Internet.

My social activities have stopped for now. I'm careful since I'm in a high-risk group. It wasn't comforting when the Lieutenant Governor of Texas stated in a press conference, "Seniors, especially those seventy and older, should give their life to save the economy. No need to shut down, since it's basically affecting the older people."

Hell, I still want to enjoy life. He didn't apologize either. Since he's seventy, I wonder if he's ready to make that sacrifice.

Every time I'm tempted to go out to a restaurant or a friendly gathering, an incident occurs.

A former employee called me. I'd been trying to reach her for a month, but no response. Finally, she called, explaining she had the virus. She and her daughter were sick for three weeks. She's in her forties. She was delirious with severe diarrhea and vomiting, along with coughing so harshly she frequently urinated on herself. She went to the emergency room, and they sent her home because she didn't have a fever. The doctor instructed her to quarantine for fourteen days, take Tylenol for the pain, and get some rest. She never had a fever throughout the whole ordeal. Her daughter's illness wasn't as severe—she only lost her sense of smell and taste. She said it was the worst experience of her life. You can also catch it again if you're not careful. Of course, I stayed in the house.

My savior is my writing, which stimulates me and keeps me busy. There's only so much television you can watch. It's been six months now, with no end in sight. I take it one day at a time, which helps me stay calm. It's like we're living in the Twilight Zone or starring in a bad science-fiction movie. This is surreal.

I'll be honest, temptation got the best of me. I went to the dentist, a friendly gathering, and the beauty shop. After each outing, I quarantined myself for fourteen days. None of us have ever experienced anything like the virus, which makes you a shut in. I envy those people who just go on with their lives, not worrying about the consequences. They do what they want to do when they want to do it.

Living alone in this pandemic is challenging, but it's not going to beat me down. Sometimes I take a slow drive to the car wash or go get gas for the car. Whenever I feel sad, I think about my ancestors and what they endured. I figured that prisoners do ten, twenty, thirty years, or life in jail. Surely, I can shelter in place, wash my hands, and try to live another day.

Oops, don't forget that damn mask. I don't like it one bit, but I wear it whenever I leave the house. Anyway, you can't enter most places without one on. Even with all this going on, life is still good.

The Front

I'M A MACHO TYPE OF GUY who likes to win in all areas of life. Most things are a contest for me to dominate my opponent. I enjoy a good time—smoking weed, drinking whiskey, and flirting with the ladies. I'm an insurance agent for State Farm, one of their top producers. I played football in college, which is an excellent conversation tool with clients. I'm a smooth operator with the ladies, too, due to my charm, along with good looks. I'm forty-two and divorced, with two grown girls spoiled by their daddy.

My buddy Rico had a birthday party, along with celebrating Black History Month, which is an annual event. It's a fun time with plenty of women for the picking.

This sister walked in. Her fine brown frame caught my attention right away. She was looking good in a blue dress that fit her like a glove. You could tell she worked out; her curves look good in all the right places. She had a dazzling smile with full, kissable lips. I wanted her. I walked over to her, crooning, "Hi, darling. My names Wayne Evans, at your service."

She replied, "Hello, I'm Vanessa Scott." As she smiled,

she shook my hand and walked off. Well, she's playing hard to get. This was going to be interesting. She ignored me the remainder of the evening. Every time I approached her, she'd smile, nod her head, and walk off. It was 2 a.m. when I saw her getting her coat to leave. I followed her outside to her car, a silver Volvo with a grey interior.

She looked surprised when I asked for her phone number. She chuckled, "I don't know you. You could be a serial killer."

I responded, "I'm a close friend of Rico's."

She grinned," I don't know Rico. I was invited by Harriet, who didn't show up, but I still had a good time."

I begged, "Please give me your number. I'd like to get to know you better. Honest, I'm an okay dude." She laughed and gave me her business card as she drove off.

I called her for two weeks with no response, but the third week she answered the phone. She explained that she'd been out of town on a case in her position as a postal inspector. She was friendly as we talked for thirty minutes. We agreed to meet at noon on Saturday at Starbucks in Hyde Park. I didn't know where she lived, but Hyde Park was good. Hell, President Obama has a home in the area.

I got there early to secure good seats by the window. Vanessa was on time, looking good in a red dress with matching earrings. The time flew by as we shared information about ourselves. She was thirty-five and divorced with no children. My kind of woman—an independent professional woman who can take care of herself.

While she was talking, I visualized her naked in bed with me. I asked her for a dinner date, and she accepted. I took her to dinner at Norms, a Black-owned restaurant featuring jazz on Saturday nights. We had a good time, scheduling another date the following week. Sometimes she paid for dinner when we went out. Vanessa was a classy lady, an excellent cook with a spotless condo.

It was two months before we had sex. Although she took the pill, she still made me use a condom, which meant she didn't trust me. I didn't like using condoms; sex was better without it. But she was stubborn in refusing my requests. We became a couple, spending most of our time together. Vanessa loved to entertain during the holidays, hosting excellent parties and serving her good home cooking. I liked most of her friends, especially one that worked for the IRS; she was funny as hell.

We'd been dating about two years when I decided that Vanessa was wife material. First, I had to train her to understand her role in this relationship. I'm the leader, and she's to follow my direction. She's too independent for her own good. I'm a good catch for many women wanting a tall, handsome, professional man like myself.

It became time to execute my plan of action and show her who's boss. I arranged several dates and cancelled at the last minute. To make her jealous, I made sure that some of her friends saw me with another woman and would tell her. Vanessa wanted marriage and a baby, which I'd give her if she acted right. She was thirtyseven, and time was running out. I discussed our future together but needed proof of her commitment by having sex without a condom, getting a key to her condo, and moving in with her to save money to pay off some bills. I gave her a month to think about it, knowing she'd miss me like crazy. Women are desperate for men like me.

It was a month later when she invited me over for dinner. I was feeling smug and triumphant. Vanessa blurted out, "I've met someone else this past month.

I can't see you anymore. It's obvious that you're not satisfied with this relationship. Now is your chance to find someone who can make you happy."

I was stunned—this caught me by surprise. I was livid. How could she do this to me? Don't you know I love you?" I said. "You're the only woman for me. I was going to marry you. I was only pretending not to care." She stared at me in disbelief. I pleaded, "Please, please, give me another chance. My acting nonchalant was just a front. Darling, I need you!"

She sighed; "Honestly, by your actions, I didn't think you cared anymore. I'm so sorry, but it's over between us."

I sat at her kitchen table and sobbed uncontrollably. She said, trying to smile. "We can still be friends."

Poetry Musings Old and New

WARNING

Lost in love,
Hard to see,
Immersed in you,
Where is Me?

OPEN SEASON

Inside my home.
Outside in the fresh air,
An innocent jog in the neighborhood,
A trek to the store. It doesn't seem to matter,
 As profiling, bias, and suspicion stalks me,
Alas a violent act ensues,
As death wraps me tightly in its embrace.

SHARING

Everyone wants a piece of my big toe,
It's my toe and belongs to me,
I don't want to share it anymore,
Get your own toe and let me be,
'Cause my big toe is just for me.

ANTICIPATION

Hair is graying,
Steps are slower.
Heart is heavier,
Hopes have diminished.
Eyes are bright as light,
Smile is radiant as fire.
Take my hand,
So we can go together.

NIGHTMARE

The virus is here,
Survival is the harsh reality,
Secluded alone in my home,
Member of a high-risk group is my offense,
Fear grows with time,
When will it be safe again for my kind?

About the Author

Zenobia Orimoloye grew up in Chicago, Illinois, in one of the oldest Black communities in America, Morgan Park. She's lived in Chicago, Milwaukee, Knoxville, Cincinnati, Detroit, and Austin. In 2018 she performed in a show sponsored by Austin's Fuse Box Festival called "All the Sex I've Ever Had." She's listed in "Two Thousand Notable American Women" in the American Biographical Institute. Impressions is her fifth book, following Passages (up close and personal short stories), Reflections (short stories of memorable moments), Choices (thirteen short stories) and Bits of Pieces (sixteen poems and four short stories). She's written three plays: Brothers, Deception, and The Visit. Zenobia's work has been broadcast on KUT-FM, Austin's NPR affiliate. She is a graduate of Loyola University and a retired civil servant who currently lives in Austin, Texas